SYSTEMA PARADOXA

ACCOUNTS OF CRYPTOZOOLOGICAL IMPORT

SUPPLEMENTARY VOLUME 1
CRYPTID COMPENDIUM
2021 TO 2025

AS COMPILED BY DANIELLE ACKLEY-MCPHAIL
ILLUSTRATED BY JW HARP

NEOPARADOXA
Pennsville, NJ
2026

PUBLISHED BY
NeoParadoxa
A division of eSpec Books
PO Box 242
Pennsville, NJ 08070
www.especbooks.com

ISBN: 978-1-965266-10-6

Interior Design: Danielle McPhail, McP Digital Graphics

Cover Art: JW Harp
Cover Design: Mike and Danielle McPhail, McP Digital Graphics
Interior Illustrations: JW Harp

Copyediting: Greg Schauer and John L. French

Dedication

To all of our authors
—past, present, and future—
for bringing this series to life

The Systema Paradoxa Series

Lest anyone misconstue our intent here, this is by no means a comprehensive compendium of all cryptids, merely those we have featured in the first five years of the Systema Paradoxa series.

With luck—and good fortune—we will be bringing you a second compendium in another five years.

Contents

artist's rendition of a Batsquatch

BATSQUATCH

ORIGINS: First sighted after the eruption of Mount St. Helens, this cryptid seems centralized to the Pacific Northwest, with sightings primarily in the Cascade Mountains, Washington State, and California, but also reaching as far east as Ohio. However, there are noted accounts of flying primates going back as far as the sixteenth century all around the world. There is a marked similarity to these cryptids despite regional variation in names.

DESCRIPTION: While accounts vary, most agree this is a flying primate with blue fur and red or yellow eyes. The muzzle resembles that of a wolf, while the ears are batlike. It is also said to have bird-like feet. All accounts make mention of very sharp teeth.

Batsquatch (a melding of the words 'bat' and 'Sasquatch') stands between seven and nine feet tall and its leather-like wings have a fifty-foot wing span, with which it is able to fly very, very fast.

Another unusual trait ascribed to the Batsquatch is the ability to psychically interfere with technological items such as car engines and transmission devices, like televisions and radios.

LIFE CYCLE: Unknown.

HISTORY: The earliest recorded account of a Batsquatch sighting occurred in March 1980, in the aftermath of the eruption of Mount St. Helens.

Perhaps the creature awoke from a form of hibernation or the natural disaster dislodged the Batsquatch from a previously self-contained habitat.

These theories, of course, have yet to be substantiated.

Throughout the '90s all the way until recent days, there have been encounters with this powerful creature. These sightings have happened with sufficient regularity that some people in the region caution about going out after dark.

In 1994, a young man was driving in Pierce County, Washington, when something caused his engine to stall. When he got out to check, a large creature landed on the hood, buckling it. When he looked, he found himself face to face with a snarling Batsquatch. He fled, reaching town with the back of his shirt shredded. When the vehicle was retrieved, the hood was dented and scratched, as if by clawed feet.

As recently as June 2021, a dawn encounter took place as a young woman hiking with her dog came face to face with this living legend on a trail in Ape Canyon (the site of a famous 1924 encounter where miners were besieged in their cabin one night by multiple Sasquatches.)

Both the woman and her dog survived the encounter, but this and other events have experts wondering if decreased human activity is drawing out these and other cryptids, or have secret experiments encroached on their territory and driven them back into the public eye?

VARIATIONS: The Ahool (Java), Ropen (New Guinea), Camazotz (Mesoamerica), and Orang Bati (Southeast Asia).

artist's rendition of the Beast of Busco

BEAST OF BUSCO

(Also known as Oscar)

ORIGINS: In 1898, near Churubusco, Indiana, a local farmer reported sighting a giant turtle in the lake on his farm. No further note was taken on the matter until fifty years later when two local men went fishing on the lake and likewise reported sighting the turtle, estimating it to be at least five hundred pounds, larger than any known specimen.

DESCRIPTION: Said to be longer than ten feet, with a shell the size of a car top and a head as large as a child, the Beast of Busco is estimated to weigh over a quarter of a ton. Given the descriptions, the theory is that the Beast—affectionately named Oscar after the farmer who originally reported him and who owned the farm and lake it is said to call home—is a rather large specimen of alligator snapper. While this species averages forty to seventy pounds, one has been recorded at 236 pounds, and there is an unverified account of one weighing 403 pounds, documented in Kansas in 1937.

LIFE CYCLE: alligator snappers can live up to four hundred years, gaining an estimated one pound a year. Though primarily found in warmer regions, as they age they tend to move to more northern climes, lending some faint veracity to the possibility of one making its way to Indiana.

HISTORY: First encountered in 1898, Oscar would not be sighted again until 1948 by two locals fishing in the lake he purportedly calls home. Then again, soon after, by the farmer who now owned the property.

The report was picked up by the local newspaper and somehow went national, with reporters and spectators coming in droves to witness the farmer's efforts to trap the Beast of Busco, going to more and more extreme efforts, from attempting to drain the lake to sending in a deep-sea diver and even dredging. The farmer became obsessed, devising all sorts of traps, only to have them fail. There were more sightings, however, including one in 1949 where two hundred spectators saw the turtle surface in an attempt to consume a duck being used as bait.

Though Oscar was never captured, the town embraced him as their own and celebrate his legend with a four-day event called Turtle Days each year.

BEAST OF GEVAUDAN

ORIGINS: Said to be active between 1764 and 1767 in the region Gevaudan, France, there were many theories as to the nature of the beast, purported to be a were-wolf, a shape-shifting sorcerer, or a somehow-surviving prehistoric beast. Dedicated hunts are said to have ended the beast's reign of terror, but agreement as to the nature of the creature or creatures have never been reached. It is believed there was likely at minimum a breeding pair, and perhaps young.

DESCRIPTION: Accounts of the beast vary wildly, enough so that sources agree there must have been more than one despite the cryptid's singular name. It is a vicious creature said to move on all fours, roughly the size of a cow or horse. The coloring is reported either as solid red or as red with a grey patch or stripes down the back, though some accounts describe it as not being red at all, rather with black and white patches all over. Witnesses claimed it had the features of a bear, wolf, hyena, and panther all at once, with small round ears close to the head and a long snout lined with large teeth. It was said to have a long, strong neck, and an equally long and strong tufted tail, which it used whip-like to attack its prey. It was known to ambush its prey, seizing it by the neck and even decapitating its victims. Accounts depict it with either split hooves or hoof-like tips to each toe, while others posited that the creature's claws were simply heavy and thick enough to resemble hooves. The other distinctive feature cited is that the beast was believed to be impervious to normal bullets.

Given the length of time since these documented attacks, written accounts are all we can go on. Based on those, however, crypto-zoologists theorize the beast was either a new variant or a hybrid of existing animals, or a prehistoric species such as a Bear-dog, Dire Wolf, or Hyaenodon, that somehow survived unnoticed. Another theory is that the creature could potentially be a member of an extinct group of hooved predators called mesonychids, based on even earlier accounts from the regions of Armenia and Assyria.

LIFE CYCLE: Unknown, although some accounts document a mated pair traveling with grown young.

HISTORY: Over the three years of documented attacks allegedly by the Beast of Gevaudan, nearly one hundred deaths are attributed

artist's rendition of a Beast of Gevaudan

to the creature, along with a number of unsuccessful attacks. Primarily known for attacking solitary people, mostly but not exclusively women and children, there are accounts of the beast attacking and being driven off by groups.

One such attack upon a group of children, successfully repelled by ten-year-old Jacques Portefaix, resulted in the boy being given a bounty by the King and an education paid for by the crown. At one point there was a 6,000-livre bounty on the creature's head, resulting in many attempts to hunt it. The attacks went on for two more years, though several creatures believed to be the beast were killed over that time. In June of 1767 Jean Chastel was reported to have shot a wolf-like creature with a silver bullet. The stomach of the slain beast contained human remains and the creature had characteristics not found in wolves. No clear identification was made of the beast's nature, but the killings did cease, giving credence to the fact that was the beast.

artist's rendition of Bessie, The Lake Erie Monster

BESSIE
THE LAKE ERIE MONSTER

(Also referred to as South Bay Bessie, The Lake Erie Monster, Great Snake of Lake Erie, and Knock-off Nessie)

ORIGINS: A regional cryptid similar to the Loch Ness Monster, also referred to as Nessie, and Champy of Lake Champlain's fame, Bessie is said to inhabit Lake Erie, which borders on New York, Pennsylvania, Ohio, Michigan, and Canada. There have been documented sightings up and down the coast for over one hundred thirty years.

However, legends of a lake monster in the area predate these recorded cases. Tribes in the region, particularly the Iroquois, have long told tales of Oniare, a horned dragon-like snake that also calls the Great Lakes home.

Though sharing the singular moniker of Bessie, some believe there to be a population of these creatures living in the lake, which supports the highest fish production in the Great Lakes. This would account for the scope and variations of the reports.

DESCRIPTION: Generally cited as a long, snake-like creature averaging about one to two feet in diameter (though some accounts have reported as much as four) and between fifteen and sixty feet long. Bessie is said to have four flippers and a flat tail, but accounts vary as to whether her head is shaped like a dog's, snake's, or horse's.

There is also some variation in reported coloration, ranging from silver or grey to copper-like to greenish-brown or black.

Several accounts describe the creature's body as cigar or sturgeon-shaped and reptilian, and some even claim the creature has arms.

The scientific community have proposed several possible explanations for the reported activity, including a population of creatures related to either the Plesiosaur or Ichthyosaurus or in the case of the swimmers inexplicably bitten, Blowfin, a species of highly aggressive, prehistoric-looking fish with strong jaws and well-developed teeth.

LIFE CYCLE: Unknown, though it is theorized that several unexplained attacks on swimmers in Lake Erie could be the result of young Bessies learning how to feed.

HISTORY: The first sighting of a Bessie was reported in 1793, near Sandusky, Ohio. The captain of the sloop *Felicity* startled the creature when shooting at some ducks. Several more incidents occurred on the waters, with some of the sailors firing muskets on the creature, to no effect.

In 1817, two French brothers happened upon a Bessie apparently in its death throes. They fled at the sight, but later returned only to find the remains swept out to sea in their absence, leaving behind only sand disturbed by the creature's thrashing and a handful of silvery scales the size of a half-dollar.

Several witnesses over the years have spied this cryptid jumping about in the waters of the lake, either in seeming combat with some unseen creature below or playfully.

Bessies do not seem to have a fear of humans, with many reports of them coming quite close to observers, sometimes aggressively, other times not.

The natives of the region have embraced their local legend, honoring it in the naming of their sports teams and even their microbrews. Bessie has even been immortalized in road-side sculptures and made cameos in children's cartoons.

Not everyone, however, seems quite enamored with the Lake Erie Monster. There are reports of a local marina offering a 100,000-dollar reward for Bessie... dead or alive.

Bigfoot

(Also known as Sasquatch, Yeti, Skunk Ape, and various other names worldwide.)

Origins: These creatures are theorized to be descended from Gigantopithecus, a prehistoric ape once found on the Asian continent.

Accounts have been documented all over North America and worldwide, though a large percentage of sightings come from the Pacific Northwest.

Description: Bigfoot is a classification, with individual species names and descriptions varying by region. They are hirsute humanoids ranging in height from six to ten feet tall, with fur ranging from white to reddish brown to black, depending on region. Their characteristic big feet can range from one to two feet long and are said to be about one third wider than the typical human foot. Primarily, prints have been said to have five toes, but there have been claims of prints found with anywhere from two to six toes, occasionally including claws. Facial features are similar to great apes, with large eyes, prominent brows, and large, low forehead. The head is characterized by a crest and is rounded.

Life Cycle: Unknown. However, some witness testimony cites that these creatures live in family groups similar to apes.

History: Native American tribes have long had legends about bigfoot-type creatures, documented by cave paintings depicting them, but the earliest written account was in 1811. David Thompson encountered the Spokanes while mapping the wilds of Canada and North America. This tribe shared tales of hairy giants in the mountains that stole both salmon and people, on occasion. This account was the first mention of the infamous footprints.

In support of these accounts, a miner named Albert Ostman shared many decades later how he was carried off in his sleep in 1924 by a family of Sasquatch, which is behavior seen in modern apes as well.

Also in 1924, in the region of Mt. St. Helens, a group of prospectors had an encounter with a group of bigfoots that turned rather violent. After one of their party fired on a solitary creature earlier in the day, the party found themselves besieged that night, with multiple bigfoots roaring in the night and casting big rocks against the walls of the prospectors' sturdy log cabin.

In the morning, the men went to sneak away, only to encounter

artist's rendition of a Bigfoot

a lone bigfoot, which they shot, but no remains were ever recovered.

The most famous encounter, however, took place in 1967 when the legendary Patterson-Gimlin Film was captured near Orleans, California. There has been heated debate as to the film's authenticity, with analysis presented both supporting and refuting the claims of an actual encounter.

The scientific argument against the existence of bigfoots is the lack of resources needed to sustain a viable population of a species of that size in the region where the sightings have been documented. However, there is a faction among the scientific community that feels there is sufficient evidence to warrant further investigation.

artist's rendition of a Bunyip

BUNYIP

(Also known as Gu-ru-ngaty, Kianpraty, Banib, Mulyawonk, Yaa-loo, Dongu, Kine Pratie, Wowee-wowee, and Mirree-ulla.)

ORIGINS: Accounts of this fierce creature as a part of the native Australian fauna go back for many centuries, with depictions represented in Aboriginal cave art and purported remains displayed in Australia's museums all the way into the 19th century. It is said to be an aquatic animal living in creeks, swamps, billabongs, riverbeds lakes, and waterholes.

Many of the sightings are from the areas around Victoria, New South Wales, and South Australia, particularly Lake George and the Murray River. Written first-hand reports go back all the way to the mid-1800s.

The Aboriginal nations have at least nine regional variations of the Bunyip, all of them consistent in depicting a menacing aquatic creature with a taste for human flesh. In fact, the word Bunyip is said to translate to "devil" or "evil spirit" in the Wemba-Wemba language.

Some attribute this cryptid solely to Aboriginal folklore and mythology but modern accounts persist.

DESCRIPTION: While the nature of the Bunyip has not varied significantly until the modern day (popular media had taken away its teeth, making it into a shy, but friendly beastie aimed at entertaining children), the Bunyip's physical attributes have always wildly diverged from account to account. It is believed this is, in part, because as a water-dwelling creature few sightings have revealed more than its head and neck, but observers rarely agree even on those features.

There are primarily three head types reported: emu-, dog-, or horse-like. Some claimed crocodile-like, as well. Length varies between four and fifteen feet long, depending on the witness. It is said to range from the size of a dog to the size of a horse.

Other traits cited in the collected reports are one or two eyes, fins, flippers, horns, tusks, dark fur and/or feathers, whiskers, and prominent ears. Some say no tail; others claim it resembles a horse's. They are reported by some to have powerful hind legs on which they walk when they are on dry land, and sharp claws.

While there are other variations, for the sake of brevity, we will stop here, other than to say that two very peculiar descriptions exist that diverge from those more commonly encountered.

One extreme variation cites the Bunyip as snake-like, and another claims it is shaped like a giant starfish.

One thing all reports seem to agree on, however, is that the Bunyip is deadly, amphibious, nocturnal, with powerful musk and a terrifying roar.

LIFE CYCLE: It is said that Bunyip lay massive, pale blue eggs, allegedly in platypus nests. No other details are available.

HISTORY: Many documented reports of Bunyip sightings occurred in the mid-1800s, as naturalists and explorers began cataloging the region and the influx of European settlers increased.

The first use of the word bahnyip was printed in 1812, used to describe a creature roughly fitting accounts of this cryptid. The specific spelling, Bunyip, was first used in 1845. The first newspaper accounts featured discoveries of fossils that, when shown to Aboriginal natives, were identified as Bunyip. These were displayed for many years in the natural history museum.

In 1852, an escaped convict living among the Wathaurong people wrote in his biography of several fleeting incidents where he witnessed the Bunyip, though he could not claim to have seen the whole creature.

Similar accounts were documented in 1857 by an artist traveling down the Murray River with his mother. He included sketches of his first-hand sighting of no less than six creatures he identified as Bunyips. These are just two of many accounts associated with the Bunyip.

Those who wish to rationalize these sightings theorize that the individuals reporting the encounter have confused live sightings with various seals, cassowaries, or crocodiles; and remains with extinct marsupials such as Diprotodon, Zygomaturus, Nototherium, or Palorchestes.

artist's rendition of a Camazotz

CAMAZOTZ

(Also known as Cama-Zotz, Sotz, Zotz)

ORIGINS: While this creature has its roots in mythology as a bat spirit serving the underworld, camazotz have a history beyond the myth and is very much a presence in modern Mexico, removing it from legend and bringing it into the realm of speculation. In lore and legend, he is associated with the night, death, and sacrifice.

DESCRIPTION: Described as a massive, humanoid bat the size of a large man or bigger. Some accounts say of the vampire variety, others claim leaf-nose or spear-nose. Whatever the variety, its nose is said to be razor-sharp. The creature's skin is brown, covered in either black clothing or fur. The eyes are either black or red, and the creature has two sets of wings. It is said to have superstrength and can exhale disease over people. Some report that it can both fly and hover and as with conventional bats is a nocturnal creature.

LIFE CYCLE: Unknown.

HISTORY: Camazotz was portrayed as a servant to the gods used to punish people. He was so evil he was trapped in hell, but later released as a punishment to the Mayan race, which Camazotz is said to have destroyed. However, camazotz are also mentioned in the Popol Vuh (Book of the People) as large bat-like monsters rather than one supernatural entity. It is possible that one was named after the other.

They were known for attacking both people and livestock, terrorizing them and sucking out their blood. As recently as the early 2000s, in the regions of Monterrey and Chihuahua, Mexico, there have been reports of encounters with this bat-like creature attacking people and cars, including that of a respected lawman, shaking the patrol car and causing the officer to crash. Camzotz are still blamed for mutilating livestock to this day.

artist's rendition of a Chesapeake Bay Sea Serpent

CHESAPEAKE BAY SEA SERPENT

(Also known as Chessie.)

ORIGINS: While theories abound as to the nature and origin of this cryptid—rationalized as everything from anaconda to manatee to oar fish and even a dinosaur that survived the meteor impact—accounts have remained on a whole consistent and no one has posited where it has come from, only that it has called the Bay its home since at least 1846.

DESCRIPTION: Cited as a dark-toned serpentine or eel-like creature with a head the size of a football and the shape of either a horse or a deer. Accounts vary on the length, ranging between ten and forty feet, with a girth similar to a telegraph pole. The eyes are described as either large and dark, or non-existent, with only dark slots where the eyes would be. Some witnesses claimed to have seen flippers, while others were adamant there were none.

LIFE CYCLE: Unknown.

HISTORY: The first accounts of this creature, understandably, hail from a sea captain sailing off the Delmarva Peninsula in 1846.

Reported sightings continue pretty regularly from there, with the most notable being in 1936 when a pilot flying a military helicopter spotted a strange creature in the waters below.

It wasn't until 1982 that the first video was captured by the hosts of a dinner party at Love Point on Kent Island. When examined by experts at the Smithsonian, they were noted as saying, "animated but undefinable." The labs at John Hopkins, however, acknowledged a definite serpentine form in the video.

The most documented activity took place between the 1970s and 1990s. The last reported sighting was in 2014.

VARIATIONS: There are legion of accounts of sea serpents from all over the world bearing similarities to Chessie, such as Loch Ness's Nessie, the Ogopogo, the Con Rit, the Manipogo, and the Lake Elsinore Monster, just to name a few.

artist's rendition of a Dingbat

DINGBAT

ORIGINS: Theorized as one of the many hoax cryptids (such as the Wunk and the Squidgicum-Squee) perpetuated by the lumberjack community to heckle newcomers and frighten off unwanted hunting activity from the forests where the they made their livelihood. The Dingbat is found in the region of the Great Lakes, particularly around Rice Lake, Wisconsin.

DESCRIPTION: A hybrid of both mammal and bird, the Dingbat has a compact, feathered body, large wings, and short, pronged antlers, appearing more owl-like than bat-like. In flight, it moves super-fast. Reports say its cry is like the whinny of a horse.

This cryptid is known to torment hunters, snatch bullets out of the air, siphon gas from their vehicles, and pull pranks to annoy them.

LIFE CYCLE: Unknown.

HISTORY: Earliest mentions of the Dingbat appear in the late 19th to early 20th century, and a stuffed specimen was supposedly displayed in a tavern in the 1950s.

DOBHAR-CHÚ

(Also known as Water Dog,
Water Hound, Sea Dog,
Irish Crocodile, King of Otters,
Father of Otters, Dobarcu,
Doyarchu, Dhuragoo,
Dorraghow, or Anchu.)

ORIGINS: The first documented account of this creature in Ireland was in 1722 at Glenade Lough, near the town Creevelea. Oral tradition, however, speaks of tales going back to ancient times. More modern sightings have been reported on Achill Island, west of County Mayo, Omey Island in Connemara, and near Portumna in County Galway.

DESCRIPTION: As with the common otter, the dobhar-chú is partial to the water, found near lakes, rivers, coasts, and waterways of Ireland. Though similar in appearance to its smaller relative, with an elongated neck and sleek, lean body, the dobhar-chú can be between seven and fifteen feet in length. It is said to have some doglike features, while other accounts claim it is actually half dog and half fish. Accounts vary, some saying that it has a dark pelt, and others, a white pelt with black-tipped ears and a shape like a black cross on its back. It is also said to have orange flipper-like feet that are extensively webbed. It is capable of great speeds on land and in the water, and is said to be bloodthirsty and territorial, with a taste for human flesh.

By some folkloric accounts, there is a variation of the dobhar-chú with a long horn on its head. Those who have witnessed this creature report vocalizations of an unusual hissing sound, and also a haunting screech.

In some encounters, it has been said that the dobhar-chú has been accompanied by as many as one hundred conventional otters, which has garnered it the title of King, or Father, of Otters.

Lore and legend claim that this creature's fur is magical, with the power to protect the bearer from harm.

Some theorize this cryptid is related to the prehistoric Siamogale melilutra, which dates to over six million years ago, was purportedly the size of a wolf, and weighed over one hundred pounds. Others believe it is related to the Enhydriodon dikikae, another gigantic prehistoric creature known as the bear otter.

LIFE CYCLE: The Dobhar-Chú live as mated pairs and are known to attack in groups of two or more. No mention is made of their young, though presumably they are born and raised as other otters are.

artist's rendition of a Dobhar-Chú

HISTORY: In 1722, a woman named Grace McGloighlin, nee Connolly, was killed by the Dobhar-Chú, and the details of her death are engraved on her tombstone. It is said that her husband Terence came upon his wife's body and the sleeping creature and killed it, avenging her death. He was subsequently pursued by the creature's mate across county Sligo. At the end of the chase, her husband is said to have killed the second Dobhar-Chú by lancing it at the base of its neck as it charged him. While there are accounts of sightings dated earlier than this, this is the most famous account.

Modern accounts continue to this day, including one in 2003 on Omey Island in Connemara by an Irish artist and his wife who were there camping. In the early hours of the morning they were woken by a strange yelping cry. When they investigated, they spied a creature as large as their Labrador retriever swimming across the lake. It emerged and reared up on its hind legs to stand at least five foot tall before disappearing back into the water.

Similar creatures have been reported in Scotland, at Loch Gairloch and the Inner Hebrides Island of Skye as far back as 1510 and 1703, as well as a plethora of other water monsters.

There are other supersized otters known to exist, such as the South American giant otter (saro Pteronura brasiliensis), and the North Pacific sea otter (Enhydra lutris), but none lay claim to such lore and legend.

artist's rendition of a Dwayyo

DWAYYO

(Also known as Dewayo, Hexenwolf, Snarly Yow)

ORIGINS: Accounts of this cryptid first appear in Frederick County dating back as early as the 1920s and '30's, but could date back as far as the 1700s, believed by some to be related to the Dutch hexenwolf. German settlers of the region counted the dwayyo as protection against the snallygasters (their natural enemy) thus the painting or hanging of hex signs on buildings in the community to this day. Other accounts cite them as the earliest occurrence of dogmen.

DESCRIPTION: These are bipedal creatures ranging in height from four to eight feet tall or more. Some accounts cite them as the size of a deer, others, the size of a bear. There have been reports of them running on all fours, but their general stance is noted as upright. They have canine or wolf-like features, bushy tails, and long hair. Their coats can be a range of colors: black, dark brown, grey, fawn, or brindle, sometimes with stripes on their lower section. Some reports note powerful legs, muscular like a kangaroo's. Their cries are most described as growling like a wolf or a dog, or horrid screams.

LIFE CYCLE: Little is known about the life expectancy of dwayyo or the stages of their life. It is known that they are pack animals. They are photo-phobic and avoid bright light and thus are usually nocturnal hunters.

HISTORY: As early as the 18th century, there have been accounts of bipedal wolf-like creatures in Frederick County, in particular the areas of West Middleton and Wolfsville.

The first mention specifically attributed to dwayyo is from 1944, and is limited to frightful screams and footprints in West Middleton. The period of greatest activity and reported first-hand encounters occurred in the 1960s and '70s, near Gambrill State Park, Route 77, and Cunningham Falls State Park.

In December 1965, around one hundred local college students signed up to hunt the dwayyo, but none of them showed up at the scheduled time. There continue to be reported sightings as recently as 2020, though some claim the dwayyo have shifted their territory closer to Port Deposit and the Conowingo Dam.

artist's rendition of El Cadejo

El Cadejo

(From the Spanish word
"cadena" meaning "chain.")

Origins: A creature, or at times two creatures, cited in Central American folklore, primarily that of El Salvador, Belize, Costa Rica, Nicaragua, Honduras, Guatemala, and southern Mexico.

While their origin is claimed to be the result of a curse in most accounts, there are multiple variations. In the vast majority of those, there are always two cadejo: one white and one black. The white one is said to be benevolent, protecting those out late at night, particularly drunks. The black one is malicious, harrying and even harming travelers not by direct attack, but by driving them mad. There are some regional accounts where the natures of the cadejo are reversed, with the black being good and the white evil.

In other variations, there are said to be three types of black cadejo. The first is the very embodiment of the devil, appearing as a large, wounded dog with smoldering chains about its hooved feet. Rather than do harm, this one is a harbinger of misfortune.

The second variation is a vicious black dog that torments its victims before tearing into them, unless the white cadejo is nearby.

The final variation is the offspring of a normal dog and a black cadejo. This one can be killed, though with difficulty, and it does not savage its victims, but drives them mad with eerie sounds and by pounding them with its muzzle.

As mentioned, the origins of this cryptid seem rooted in myth and legend, but it bears noting that mankind has a long history of creating tall tales to explain natural occurrences, and despite the supposed magical nature of these beasts, there have been more current reports of sightings.

Description: In most accounts, the cadejo are paired, one white beast and one black, but sometimes there is just one, and if so, that one is the black cadejo. They have the appearance of wolves or dogs, but as big as a cow, with the horns and hooves of goats or, in some accounts, bulls. They are said to smell either strongly of goat, or like the stench of urine combined with sulphur. Some say that they have burning red eyes, or that the black cadejo is red-eyed, and the white cadejo is either blue-, green-, or golden-eyed. It is believed that if you meet their gaze, you will be unable to move.

Life Cycle: Though some regions believe it is possible for cadejo to breed with common dogs, details on their development remain unavailable. It is noted that such offspring bear a similar demeanor to their cryptid parent, as well as being nearly as difficult to kill. When one has been dispatched, the body puts off a foul odor before dissolving into nothing, leaving behind a stain on the earth from which nothing will grow thenceforth.

HISTORY: The most common legend of el cadejo speaks of two brothers traveling through the wilderness. They stop at the home of a black magician. In exchange for food and a place to stay the night, they agree to collect wood for the magician's fire. In the morning, when the man sees that they didn't not honor their agreement, he casts a curse upon them as they leave, harrying them with voices and sounds until they turn away, then changing them into beasts according to their nature. Thus cursed, they are cast out from their home and forced to wander, driven by the curse to help or harm travelers.

To this day, truckers have reported these cryptids along the highways up through Texas, and there are el cadejo sightings as far as the hills of Lake Elsinore, in Southern California.

GLAWACKUS

(Also known as the Northern Devil Cat, Granby Panther, Injun Devil, Glastonbury-What-Is-It)

ORIGINS: First sighted in Glastonbury, Connecticut, there have been accounts of this creature throughout the region, though it mostly lives on through the lore and legends of lumberjacks and timbermen who frequent the remote territories where the Glawackus is said to lurk.

DESCRIPTION: Accounts vary as to the description of this creature, some citing it as a large cat, others a large dog, and still others beyond that claiming it is a melding of both feline and canine, though there is some disagreement as to which portions of the animal are which. Popular belief, however, is that the Glawackus is a melding of bear and large cat, either a panther or lion, or perhaps both. By all accounts, the beast is terrifying.

Whatever its composition, this cryptid is estimated to stand between two and two and a half feet at the shoulder and is four feet long, with a two-foot-long tail that some claim is bushy. Its fur ranges from deep black to tawny. Most accounts agree that its other defining features are glowing, ember-like eyes and a horrific screech similar to that of a hyena. Some claim that if you look into the creature's eyes, it will wipe your memory.

LIFE CYCLE: Unknown.

HISTORY: In 1939 multiple sightings of this creature were documented in the Glastonbury area over a period of months. In addition to the eyewitness accounts were reports of howling and blood-curdling screams in the night and a sharp increase in missing pets and mutilated livestock. Dogs that pursued the creature came back injured or not at all.

As the reports continued, the creature was dubbed the Glawackus, some say by a local newspaper editor, others by a Connecticut scientist. All agree that the moniker is a combination of Gla- for Glastonbury, wack- for wacky, and -us to sound suitably scientific.

Many hunting parties set out to track the creature, some caught up in the sensationalism, others with serious intent, well equipped and with hunting dogs. All attempts were unsuccessful, though it became quite the craze with at times as many as two hundred separate hunting parties invading the woods and caves as far as the Berkshires in search of the Glawackus. To this day there are

artist's rendition of a Glawackus

those who advertise the avail-ability of sighting logs to be had. Before the original fervor died down two miles worth of tracks were discovered outside of town, but no other proof was discovered.

In the 1950s a second rash of sightings took place, along with reported incidents similar to those in 1939, this time extending as far north as Granby, but those too died down in a matter of months.

THEORIES: Some believe that the creature was a puma or large cat escaped from a private collection or zoo, others believe it to be a cat fisher, a species rare in that area but very similar in description to the reported accounts right down to its terrifying scream. In the end, we can but speculate as the Glawackus continues to elude all efforts to track it down.

artist's rendition of a Goatman

GOATMAN

ORIGINS: The earliest sighting of Goatmen is recorded in 520 BC, with the satyrs of Greek myth, cited as both lusty and violent creatures. Modern accounts of this cryptid, in one version or another, are reported from multiple regions in the US including Texas, Pennsylvania, Louisiana, Florida, Michigan, Arkansas, Alabama, California, Kentucky, Indiana, and Maryland.

Lore presents two possible origin stories for the Maryland variant of this cryptid, with some details echoed in other regions.

Some say it began with a goatherder driven crazy with rage when local teenagers killed his flock.

Others believe Goatman began as a scientist from the Beltsville Agricultural Research Center who experimented on goats. Something went wrong, turning him into a completely insane half-man, half-goat who reportedly wanders the area at night attacking cars with an axe.

DESCRIPTION: Said to be between six to eight feet tall, this cryptid has been described either as a hairy humanoid with the face of a man, or a man with the horns, legs, and hooves of a goat. The eyes are said to be red and the body powerful, but deformed.

Goatman is also known for being angry, aggressive, and blood-thirsty, making a high-pitched shrieking sound, and a having a pungent odor. He is said to possess the strength of two grown men and wield an axe. He is also noted for being territorial.

This cryptid is said to live under bridges and in caves in more rural areas

LIFE CYCLE: Unknown.

HISTORY: While there have been stories of some type of Goatman for a very long time and from different regions, the accounts bear much similarity.

In some, Goatman is said to roam the night, attacking those parked in out-of-the-way places making out, luring away the male and killing him brutally with his axe, and then hanging him above the car to torment the female hiding within.

In other tales of the Goatman, he is said to mutilate local livestock and kill small animals, particularly dogs, beheading them or cleaving them in half. Often the body is never found.

There have been many sightings throughout the years, mostly

of Goatman disappearing into wooded areas, and in some accounts of attacks on animals, there have been distinctively hooved footprints found near the remains.

VARIATIONS: Grunch, Waterford Sheepman, Pope Lick Monster, Proctor Valley Monster, Lake Worth Monster, Satyr, Faun, Krampus.

GUGWE

(Also known as Face Eater
or Head Eater.)

ORIGINS: Said to inhabit dense and remote boreal forests in Canada, primarily Quebec and Labrador, though also reported in the Northwestern territories, where Gugwe activity is so pronounced there is a region called Headless Valley, or Valley of the Headless Men.

There is some theory that they are aquatic adaptation of Bigfoot due the number of sightings near bodies of water and a claimed fondness for fish.

There have been encounters reported in North America, primarily in Wisconsin, but also in the Appalachian Mountains and as far south as Texas.

DESCRIPTION: Accounts depict the Gugwe as a humanoid creature between six to eight feet tall, with fur ranging from white to grey to black, though a few accounts cite them as having red fur, in full or part.

Gugwe's most distinctive physical characteristics are a sagittal crest and protruding snout (dog-like or baboon-like) with large canines.

They have been reported to walk bipedally, but also on all fours, leaving a long track, narrow at the heel and dividing into two rounded toes at the front. Some report the toes to be webbed.

The other defining characteristics are a foul odor—some say fishlike—and its haunting, high-pitched cry.

Extremely aggressive and territorial in nature, Gugwe are reported to tear the heads off trespassers and eat them. Indigenous tribes consider them very dangerous to humans, but mostly they are believed to hunt small creatures at night.

This cryptid has been associated with many others of a similar type, such as Yeti/Sasquatch/Bigfoot, Dogmen, Woodbooger, and Wendigo, primarily because of shared features: tall, furred, humanoid mix, bipedal nature. Its distinct differences, however, bring the Gugwe to be classified as its own creature rather than a variant or subset of its more prominent cousins.

LIFE CYCLE: No definitive evidence has been found, and reports vary whether or not Gugwe are solitary creatures or live and travel in family groups, similar to the primates they resemble.

HISTORY: While accounts have been recorded in folklore for centuries, modern accounts do not begin until the 1900s.

artist's rendition of a Gugwe

The first documentation in writing appeared in Elliot Merrick's True North, published in 1933, recounting a young girl's harrowing encounter with a Gugwe in the Labrador region in 1913.

The creature was not captured on film until 1995, only discovered after the fact in the background of scenic shots taken in Seven Chutes, Quebec. Other accounts have been reported, with the most recent being in 2012, primarily from hikers.

While some theorize that the Gugwe is an escaped scientific experiment from either Canada or the US, there is no evidence to substantiate these claims.

artist's rendition of a J'ba Fofi

J'BA FOFI

(Also known as Congolese Giant Spiders)

ORIGINS: Initially cited as a denizen of the Congolese rainforests, the first documented case by a western source being in the region of Lake Nyasa, this cryptid has also been reported around the world, including Mozambique, Uganda, Papua New Guinea, Cameroon, Venezuela, Vietnam, the Amazon, England, Canada, and Louisiana and Kentucky in the United States.

DESCRIPTION: The J'ba Fofi (Congolese for very large spider) are described as massive ground-dwelling spiders similar to tarantulas or trapdoor spiders. Their coloring is generally brown with purple markings on their abdomens, which are described as the size of a basketball, and they are fanged. Their leg span is said to be between two and five feet wide, and when fully reared, the J'ba Fofi stand the height of a man. By some accounts, the spiders' bodies are somewhere between thirty and forty inches long.

As ground spiders, this cryptid is said to dig shallow tunnels beneath the tree roots, generally along game trails, camouflaging the openings with screens of leaves. They then spin webs and trip lines in the area leading to their nest. Alternately, other accounts have these arachnids creating their lairs by weaving leaves into a shape similar to a traditional pygmy hut, paired with a strong circular web strung between two trees, also across a game trail. The strong, nearly invisible webs are reported to be between three and six feet in length. By some accounts, the web can also be emerald green, which in a rainforest is just as likely to be overlooked.

While their prey is generally small game such as birds and small forest antelope, the J'ba Fofi are said to be highly venomous, with toxins sufficient to kill a man. In defense against these arachnids, the inhabitants of the Congo avoid the webs whenever sighted and build their huts to deny easy entry, with tightly-spaced walls and steeply pitched floors.

Despite their great size and dangerous nature, the J'ba Fofi sightings have grown rare because they are considered great delicacies by the Baka and killed for food whenever encountered.

In the scientific community, there is some debate if such a creature as the J'ba Fofi could exist since the arachnid respiratory system is typically based on delicate "book-lungs" which resemble the pages of a book and would not be able to sustain such a large specimen. However, counterarguments have been made that is possible that a species of spider could evolve with an advanced respiratory system, such as the branchiostegal lung developed by the coconut crab (which has a three-foot leg span), allowing it to survive on land, or some other complex means of oxygenation that would allow specimens to grow to a greater size.

LIFE CYCLE: As with other arachnids, the J'ba Fofi are egg-layers. The eggs themselves are described as white or pale yellow and the size and shape of peanut shells, while the hatchlings are bright yellow with purple abdomen, darkening to brown as they mature.

HISTORY: The first non-native account of this cryptid was documented in the 1890s when a missionary and his men happened upon an enormous web. The men became entangled, drawing the attention of two J'ba Fofi, which then attacked. The missionary escaped but was bitten. Developing the following symptoms — chills, swelling around the bite, extreme pallor, and delirium, followed by unconsciousness — he eventually succumbed to the poison and died. No mention was made as to the fate of his men.

Accounts of sightings persist over the years, both in Africa and distant regions, some as recently as 2014. Most of these are in passing, with the spiders only glimpsed. However, in particular, they were said to be a considerable problem for both sides of the conflict in Vietnam as these arachnids are said to be drawn to water. Written and digital evidence has been documented over the years, including a video from 2013 purportedly showing a giant spider briefly captured via a night-vision camera filming a waterhole in Mozambique.

JERSEY DEVIL

(Also known as The Devil of Leeds, The Leeds Devil, Jabberwock, Woozle Bug, Kangaroo Horse, Kingowing, Flying Death, Flying Horse, Flying Hoof, and Cowbird.)

ORIGINS: Said to have been born in 1735, the thirteenth child of the Leeds family from the Pine Barrens of New Jersey.

After having already borne twelve children, Mother Leeds (Jane or Deborah, depending on the account) cursed having another when the family's situation was already precarious.

It is believed the father was Japheth or Daniel Leeds, or a British soldier who kept Mother Leeds as a mistress. Some even claim she was a witch and the babe's father the Devil.

Folklore says the child either was born a hairy creature at the offset, or born normal in all aspects, but swiftly transformed, flying up and away through the chimney. One account claims the child's transformation was the result of a gypsy curse. By any account, the Jersey Devil has been terrorizing the region ever since.

DESCRIPTION: The Jersey Devil's appearance has remained consistent in most accounts, where the creature is said to be a winged biped with a horse-like head, cloven hooves, clawed hands, and a tail. Interestingly enough, the hereditary Leeds family crest features a wyvern, a dragon-like creature with bat-like wings. As for the creature's voice, it is said to emit hissing, piercing shrieks, and terrible cries.

While these features remain generally the same, some reports cite slight variations, such as horns, a goat's head, snake's tail, forked tail, bat wings, or glowing (red) eyes.

There have also been wildly different accounts where the creature is humanoid with a deer or dog head, bird legs, or kangaroo-like body.

The reported height range spans from three and a half feet to the height of a man.

The creature is also believed to be impervious to harm, having been fired upon by guns and even artillery, without any effect.

LIFE CYCLE: According to folklore, the Jersey Devil was born human and cursed into its final form. There are no theories as to its reproduction or life span.

HISTORY: Starting in the early 18th century and continuing through the 20th century, there have been reports of the Jersey Devil

artist's rendition of a Jersey Devil

everywhere from its native Pine Barrens, all over South Jersey, up toward Trenton, and even North Jersey and Pennsylvania.

After its purported birth, accounts of hoof prints and ravaged livestock, particularly chickens, were common in the area.

In 1740, traveling missionaries exorcised the Devil from the region for one hundred years, but there were still reported sightings during that time.

Not much was documented until 1820, when Joseph Bonaparte (Napoleon's brother) was reported to have come face to face with the beast while hunting alone at his Bordentown estate.

In 1909, a rash of sightings sensationalized by the media led to what is called the Week of Terror, where Jersey Devil encounters were reported in not only New Jersey, but Pennsylvania, Delaware, and Maryland. Posses scoured the countryside, yelling, "If you're the Jersey Devil, rattle your chains," but the dogs refused to follow the tracks. In both the countryside and the towns and cities, the Jersey Devil is said to have tormented citizens, attacking trolley cars, making off with livestock, and accosting people outside social clubs. It was bad enough that many people refused to leave their homes. Schools and other places of business closed. Ministers, however, noted an increase in attendance.

Sightings were more sparce after that notable week, but they still persist over the years, with reports of Jersey Devil tracks, corpses, and photographs feeding the legend.

There are no accounts of the Jersey Devil attacking humans, but he is considered a harbinger of doom, having been sited before every major war, and it is said he will perform acts of mischief against those who hold evil thoughts.

The Philadelphia Zoo even offered a $10,000 reward for the capture of the Jersey Devil, and the Arch Museum perpetuated one of the most famous hoaxes in a bid to save itself from closure, purchasing a kangaroo from a circus, which was then painted and false wings and claws attached. It was billed as a captured Jersey Devil, but the exhibit was not sufficient to save the museum.

THEORIES: Some propose that these legends stem from mass hysteria; other believe the Jersey Devil could actually be a living pterodactyl, trapped in the limestone caves, fed on subterranean fish, and released by seismic activity.

artist's rendition of the Lizard Man of Scape Ore Swamp

LIZARD MAN
OF SCAPE ORE SWAMP

ORIGINS: Regional to Browntown and Bishopville, SC, along the edge of the Scape Ore Swamp. Though the recorded accounts begin in the late 1980s, the Creek tribe native to the area tell of encounters much further back.

DESCRIPTION: An aggressive, nocturnal humanoid creature seven feet tall, with green lizard-like skin that is moist and rough, three fingers and toes tipped with long black claws, red eyes, and snake-like scales. In the historic accounts from the Creek, the Lizard Man also possesses a tail. This cryptid is also said to have a craving for butter beans.

LIFE CYCLE: Unknown.

HISTORY: The earliest recorded account is from 1929, documenting an older encounter of the local Creek tribe telling of a band of hunters that went out into the night to smoke a bear from its tree, only the beast that lunged out was a Lizard Man. The hunters scattered, but the creature picked them off one by one, storing their bodies in its tree. When it came for the last of them, its attack woke a jaguar sleeping nearby, which attacked the Lizard Man, allowing the last hunter to escape.

The next recorded accounts occurred in the fall of 1987, mostly of vandalized cars in the area, with deep gouges in the metal like claw marks and chrome looking as if it had been chewed off.

One teenage boy got a flat tire. When he stopped to change it something thumped behind him. When the Lizard Man leapt onto the roof of the car, the boy jumped into the car and drove off, swerving to dislodge his attacker. When he arrived home, there were claw marks in his roof and the sideview mirror was torn away.

Over the following months, more reports were made. Local law enforcement ventured into the swamp, discovering long, three-toed prints in the mud, but had no direct encounter with the beast. An airman from the local base claimed to have shot the Lizard Man, providing blood and scale samples as proof, but later retracted his statement saying it was a hoax to perpetuate the local legend. Sighting and damaged vehicles continued to be reported, but dropped off as the weather grew cooler.

In 2015, someone came forth with an alleged photograph and video of the creature. In 2017, the South Carolina Emergency Management Division issued a warning for residents to use caution during the pending solar eclipse, citing the unusual darkness could trigger Lizard Man activity. Though many discount this cryptid as an urban legend or a hoax, the scientific community continues to conduct research in and around Scape Ore Swamp.

Lone Pine Mountain Devil

(Also known as California Mountain Devil, or just Mountain Devil.)

ORIGINS: Simply put, by all accounts these creatures originate from Hell. Where they have been sighted, however, is the Sierra Nevada mountain range, in the American Southwest and Northern Mexico. In particular, as the name dictates, around Lone Pine, California, and the Alabama Hills region, in the Inyo national forest.

DESCRIPTION: The Lone Pine Mountain Devil is describe as a large bat- or raptor-like creature, furred, with more than one set of wings and sharp talons. Its bite was said to be venomous, with multiple layers of fangs.

By some accounts, its wingspan is in the range of ten feet, with no mention of height.

LIFE CYCLE: Unknown.

HISTORY: tales of the Lone Pine Mountain Devil are cited from the mid- to late 19th century, and even into the early 20th, among both miners and settlers, and the native population, though no written accounts survive, and no photographs or physical remains are known to exist.

The grimmest account is from around 1878. A group of Spanish settlers — thirty-seven men, women, and children — vanished one night on the trail. They had stopped for a celebration that had gotten out of hand until they were indulging in sinful acts, lighting nearby trees on fire for light and warmth so they could continue into the night. A priest traveling among them disapproved. Father Justus Martinez separated himself from the party. When he heard frightening sounds, he watched in horror from his tent, spared as the Devils attacked and carried the offenders away.

The settlers vanished until two months later when miners discovered their rotting bodies. The priest wandered alone through the wilderness until he arrived at the Mission San Gabriel Arcangel with nothing but his clothes and a journal detailing that hellish night.

There were other similar accounts from the region with claims of whole traveling parties found with their faces and chests shredded or eaten to the bone, and the rest of their bodies left untouched. These claims continued all the way up to 1928, but after that there was little mention until 2003, when reported sightings of the creatures recommenced, but no discoveries of grisly remains.

artist's rendition of a Lone Pine Mountain Devil

Some believe that these creatures are guardians or protective spirits, attacking only those who destroy nature or disturb the peace of the wilderness, as several key factors in the stories told involved such behavior.

Variations: It is believed by some that the Lone Pine Mountain Devil is related to the Jersey Devil.

artist's rendition of a Mantis Man

MANTIS MAN

ORIGINS: Recent documented accounts of this cryptid are primarily in the area of the Musconetcong River in New Jersey, around Hackettstown, though some accounts place a similar creature in the region of the Thames River in New London, Connecticut, as well as an undocumented sighting in Montana.

In addition, there are ancient accounts of mantis men going back to Mesopotamia, ancient Egypt, southern Africa, and ancient Iran. Some believe them to be gods, others, aliens, and yet others, psychotropic hallucinations brought on by mind-altering herbs or ingestibles used in religious rituals.

More recent opinion theorizes there are multiple mantis creatures, genetic experiments or specimens from a breeding program that have grown beyond the scientists' ability to control and have either escaped or been released into the wild.

DESCRIPTION: While resembling a praying mantis, these have been described as definitely humanoid creatures with mantis features. By accounts, they range between two and eight feet tall, dependent on the account, with coloration ranging between brown, grey, green, and black. Some also claim the creature is translucent.

They are described as having wings, like mantises do, and mandibles, with thin, elongated limbs and the iconic triangular head with large oval eyes of both a praying mantis and an alien grey, leading to the belief they could also be extraterrestrial in origin.

It has been theorized that this cryptid may also have some form of psychic communication, which is why some sensitives have been able to spy the creature despite its ability to camouflage.

LIFE CYCLE: Unknown.

HISTORY: Most of the sightings of Mantis Man take place between 2009 and 2011. The most famous account is of two brothers fly fishing on the M'cong River. The brothers were fifty feet apart when one brother caught movement from the corner of his eye. They locked gazes briefly before the Mantis Man vanished. In a separate encounter, another individual noted a humming sound before the creature vanished. There have also been several sightings by drivers passing beside various rivers, something that is a bit peculiar as praying mantises are not known for habitating near water, being more common in the forest and among trees.

Mongolian Death Worm

(Also known as Olgoi-Khorkhoi)

Origins: Long known among the nomadic tribes of the Gobi desert, who name it Olgoi-Khorkhoi, or "large intestine worm," this cryptid hails specifically from that region. Though the desert encompasses 500,000 miles, this burrowing Worm is reported to inhabit the western or southern regions, where the desert is the most desolate.

Description: While there is some debate if this creature is, in fact, a worm, it is described as the shape of a sausage, with either a pink, blood red, or dark crimson color skin, no visible eyes or ears, and spikes protruding from either end of its body. Specimens are said to range between two and seven feet long. As worms absorb oxygen through their skin, it is theoretically possible for them to grow to the immense size reported for the Death Worm.

Among its natural defenses are the ability to spit an acidic poison or strike out with an electric discharge, both capable of killing an adult human instantly. The Worm itself is said to be poisonous to the touch and its acid is corrosive, leaving everything it touches a corroded yellow color. These creatures travel underground, leaving no more than a tell-tale wave pattern in the sand above, but are said to surface more often during the rainy period, in June and July.

Some theorize that the Mongolian Death Worm is not a worm, which would not be expected to survive the harsh environs of the desert, but perhaps a new species of worm-lizard, reptiles also known for burrowing. However, there is precedence for sand-dwelling worms, such at the Australian beach worm, to lend credence to a desert-dwelling species.

Others believe sightings are the result of hallucinations or misidentification of various species of snakes of similar description, such as the pit viper, rat snake, or sand boa. Some have even suggested these are accounts of a type of skink, though that theory is discounted as skinks have legs and scaled skin. All speculation is based on second- and third-hand accounts.

Life Cycle: Unknown.

History: Due to Soviet control of the region until 1990, there is little knowledge of the Death Worm in the west. Since then, there have been many expeditions in search of this creature or evidence of its existence, but to date, none of

artist's rendition of a Mongolian Death Worm

them have been successful. However, there are those in the field of cryptozoology who have not ruled out the existence of the Mongolian Death Worm, due to the vastness of its habitat, as well as the number of reported sightings and strange deaths. Many believe this cryptid to be more than just legend, though more concrete evidence is needed to satisfy the scientific community.

artist's rendition of a Montauk Monster

MONTAUK MONSTER

(Also known as Monty.)

ORIGINS: Theories abound about this creature, ranging from the proposition that it is a hoax to claims it is a mutant product of scientific experimentation. The most common belief is that the discovery was nothing more than a decomposing mammal whose remains were distorted by prolonged submersion in sea water. Some believe that the truth has been covered up in a conspiracy of lies. As the only evidence is photographic, all theories remain speculation.

DESCRIPTION: While primarily representing as mammalian, the Montauk Monster is distinguished by a beaked upper jaw, with pointed teeth along the lower. Other features include fur, a long tail, and flat paws tipped with nail-like claws.

LIFE CYCLE: Unknown.

HISTORY: The original remains were discovered in 2008 by three girls walking along the Ditch Plain Beach. The girls photographed the creature, but before anyone could be called in to identify the animal, another individual purportedly removed the remains to a friend's property with the intention of giving the bones to a local artist to be included in an exhibition. When approached for confirmation, the gentleman in question reported that someone had stolen the body.

Despite significant media interest, most parties involved remain closed-mouthed, leading to the speculation that the hoax or conspiracy theories may not be far from the mark.

It is believed by some that the creature was an escaped mutant from the nearby Plum Island laboratory, which studies animal disease.

Yet others claim the corpse is nothing more than a racoon, pitbull, coyote, or de-shelled turtle, though there are reasons each of these classifications is not perfectly matched with the evidence.

After the 2008 discovery, there have been multiple discoveries of Montauk Monster remains worldwide, but no definitive identification as no living specimen has been observed.

artist's rendition of a Mothman

MOTHMAN

ORIGINS: First sighted in Point Pleasant, West Virginia. There are various theories of its origin, such as an undiscovered species, an extraterrestrial being, a supernatural creature, or harbinger of catastrophe. Other sightings have been reported world-wide, including Chicago and as far away as Moscow.

DESCRIPTION: Despite the name, this humanoid creature is described with more avian features, believed to more closely resemble an owl than a moth. It is said to be slender and male, standing between six and seven feet tall. The wings are reported as white or brown with a span of ten to fifteen feet. Those who have experienced first-hand encounters have no details of the creature's features other than the eyes, which are large and red, glowing like a reflector. The eyes are also reported to be hypnotic. Its body coloration is described as white or brown or black, but mostly dark. While not very agile on the ground, moving with an awkward walking gait, Mothman is said to be able to take flight like a helicopter and fly at a rate of a hundred miles an hour.

LIFE CYCLE: Unknown.

HISTORY: In November of 1966, reports started to come in of a flying humanoid creature seen in the region of Point Pleasant, West Virginia. The first account was by the owner of a missing German Shepherd that disappeared after chasing after two glowing red eyes in the forest. After that, on the night of the 15th two young couples were out driving on route 62 near the abandoned WWII munitions plant the locals dubbed "the TNT area," when they saw this giant winged humanoid. They sped away only to be chased by the creature, which shrieked after them.

When the local paper picked up the story over a hundred similar encounters were reported over the ensuing thirteen months. There were claims that witnesses were visited by "Men in Black" and dissuaded from sharing their experiences. The accounts died down following the collapse of the Silver Bridge, a tragedy where forty-six people lost their lives.

Popular opinion was that the creature appeared as a harbinger of the event, trying to warn the townfolk, a theory that took on global significance when those in Russia reported their own sighting in Moscow right before the 1999 apartment bombings and preceding the Chernobyl reactor melted down. Miners in Germany claimed Mothman chased them away from their shaft right before it collapsed, and two photographs circulated placing Mothman in New York during the 9/11 disaster.

Reports continued to come in over the ensuing years, though not in the volume prior to December 1967, including a photograph claimed to be the Mothman taking flight circulated in 2016, and a rash of reported sightings in Chicago in 2017.

In 2002, Point Pleasant organized the first annual Mothman Festival, which continues to this day, flooding the town with three times its normal population for one weekend in September. In 2003 the town erected a Mothman statue by artist Bob Roach, and in 2005 the Mothman Museum and Research Center opened its doors.

THEORIES: Aside from the believe that Mothman could be an extra-terrestrial or a supernatural being, those more skeptical theorize that the sightings were no more than various avians mistaken for something "other," primarily either the sandhill crane, a great blue heron, or a snowy owl, all of which are large birds with wide wingspans. And the photographs claimed to be Mothman have been dismissed as Photoshopped fakes, a bird taking flight with a kill, or a bit of loose metal hanging off a bridge. But the legend and the sightings persist.

Qalupalik

(Also Qallupilluk or Qallupilluit)

Origins: A creature of the Artic, this cryptid is said to live deep in the ocean, hunting along the shores, moving among the ice floes and perhaps even inland waterways looking for opportunities to prey upon the Inuit people. Some call this aquatic creature their version of a mermaid, said to snatch children coming too close to the shore.

Description: Though accounts cite both male and female pronouns, these cryptids are most commonly referred to in the feminine manner, described as having bright eyes, fierce teeth, long hair, and slimy greenish-blue skin with bumps and scales. Their hands are webbed and possess long, claw-like finger nails.

Despite the purity of their salty ocean home, this water-dwelling bogeyman reeks of sulfur. According to accounts, they snatch children into the water with their long, thin arms, shoving them into the pouch of their amautik, an Inuit parka usually worn by women, with a pouch on the back. It is not known for certain why they snatch children. Some believe it is to devour them, others believe they are kept as companions, and yet others believe the creature steals their life force to maintain its immortality.

In their hunt, they are said to use sound, either an ethereal hum to lure their prey or a shrill noise produced by one of their two flippers to paralyze their victims. It is also believed that they possess an ability called pilutitaminik that allows them to alter their appearance to that of a seal or a whale, or perhaps other forms.

According to lore, in its true state, this creature is invulnerable, but can be killed when transformed into another form, which clever hunters have been known to use to their advantage.

Life Cycle: the origin of this marine creature is not known nor how it reproduces, but lore says this cryptid is cursed with immortality.

History: There are accounts going back centuries of those who have lost their lives in the embrace of these native cryptids. The skeptics are of the opinion that the elders merely warn the young away from the shore to keep them from falling through thinning ice, and that the noises heard were the ice cracking and buckling. Others are certain that the water's surface hides a predator waiting for unwary children to draw within

artist's rendition of a Qalupalik

reach, betrayed only by a knocking sound traveling across the ice. But what if there is no ice? It is said that if the free-flowing water is wavy or steam rises from the surface, one of these creatures may be lurking beneath the surface.

All is not about the hunt, however. There are accounts of children willfully being surrendered to this creature by their loved ones because they could not feed them, and it was believed their lot would be better. One account has a young couple searching for one such boy, seeking to retrieve him once food was plentiful again. It is said they found him tethered by a strand of seaweed so he could not flee. They could not free him at first, but waited until dawn and were able to sever the bond.

VARIANTS: Mermaid, Siren, Kappa.

artist's rendition of a Rougarou

ROUGAROU

(Also known as Loup-Garou, Rugarou, Rugaru, Roux-ga-roux, Rugaroo, Beast of Gévaudan, Stragoi, Attakapa Wolf-Walker, or Werewolf)

ORIGINS: Accounts of this wolf man have been shared as far back as medieval times. Some cite the origin as France, having migrated to North America among colonists or those banished to Quebec, the Caribbean, or the Cajun regions of the South, centralized to Louisiana. However, accounts have been cited outside these regions, as well.

An alternate source for this cryptid is rooted locally in the history of the Attakapa tribe, whose name means "man-eater" in Chocktaw and which has been associated with legends of "Wolf-Walkers" vicious shapeshifters very much similar to the tales of the Rougarou.

DESCRIPTION: By early accounts, a Rougarou ranges from six to eight feet tall, is very muscular, and can be a man, woman, or child. It has the body of a human and the head of a dog or a wolf, with glowing yellow or red eyes and very reclusive behavior. The extremities also take on a vaguely canine appearance, with long, sharp claws and, some say, only three toes.

As with most shapeshifter lore, the Rougarou possess supernatural strength, agility, and senses. They are said to be able to see clearly in the dark, hear their prey's heartbeat, and smell its faintest scent.

One characteristic of this affliction is an insatiable thirst for human blood and a hunger for raw flesh. The outcome is that regions beset by Rougarou experience high accounts of slaughtered animals, both domesticated and wildlife, drained of their blood and torn to shreds.

More modern reports describe an aggressive, snarling man/wolf hybrid with brown or black fur that will attack anyone entering the swamp, forest, or woods, shredding its victims' flesh from bone and devouring the remains. Variations in the lore include a full transformation to the animal form.

In some accounts, Rougarou are said to become creatures other than wolves, such as rabbits, dogs, pigs, alligators, cows, and even chickens. These other forms are generally white. In some regions, it is said the Rougarou can take on any of these forms completely, almost indistinguishable from the real thing, except for unusual coloring and odd behavior. However, one thing that always remains the same is the ravenous, blood-thirsty nature.

One way that Rougarou differ from traditional werewolves is that they can change form at will rather than being dictated by the phases of the moon. They also retain intelligence and awareness.

Some say this affliction results from a witch casting a curse or one being transferred by being bitten by one cursed as a Rougarou, or gazing into one's eyes. Some variants say that a witch will turn someone into a Rougarou by first turning into a wolf themselves. There are those who believe that the affliction passes on to another when the Rougarou draws, or drinks, human blood, and others who believe it is hereditary, passing down to the third child of each generation.

Depending on the version of the legend, the curse is said to last for 101 days before it can be passed on, or it lasts a lifetime. One thing that all seem to agree upon is that the cursed becomes a ravenous beast at night and reverts to human during the day, usually weak and sickly.

Among the Catholic community, the curse is said to be brought down upon those who break the rules of Lent seven years in a row. Other legends state that the Rougarou will hunt down and kill those who do not follow the rules of Lent, feasting on the blood and flesh of sinners.

When the curse has passed on, the original host becomes human again, sickly and remaining quiet about their ordeal out of shame and the fear they will be killed as a monster. If the curse passes because the Rougarou has goaded a victim into drawing its blood, it immediately reverts to human and warns the one who broke the curse not to say anything about what happened for a year and a day, or the curse will pass on to them, and they will suffer the same fate.

Weaknesses: There are those who believe some become a Rougarou by choice, while others transform as the result of a curse. Some also believe the creature could be metaphysical, perhaps of an interdimensional or spiritual nature. Whatever the root of its origin, it is important to remember the Rougarou is still human underneath and may or may not be deserving of the curse. Killing, while possible with silver weapons or decapitation, should be a last resort.

As with any lore, there are always ways to protect yourself against the beast or to defeat them. The Rougarou has both common and unique weaknesses. As with vampires, with whom the Rougarou has been associated, this shapeshifter has the inability to count beyond twelve but a compulsion to keep trying, so scattering more than twelve items before it will keep it occupied until dawn is nigh and it must flee into the swamp. Surprisingly, they are said to fear frogs, and the caw of a crow will frighten them away. Another weapon against this cryptid is anything blessed or consecrated, such as holy water, the ashes of the previous year's palm frond, salt, or blessed communion wafers. Ritual prayers or a roaring fire are also said to keep the creature away.

Aside from these, it is said that the Romani, native medicine men, shaman, VooDoo, or HooDoo practitioners can use herbs or other means to lift the curse, and certain herbs such as wolfsbane, angelica root, rue, sage, bay leaves, and laurel can ward off the beast, but only if gathered under a waxing moon. Some in the region carry mojo bags or folded leaves of wolfsbane in their wallets.

According to lore, a silver bullet or forged blade through the heart or used to decapitate is said to kill a Rougarou, or an alloy with high silver content, but the bullet or blade must not be removed from the wound or the Rougarou will regenerate and rise again. However the beast is banished, it is important to salt and burn the remains and scatter the ashes lest they rise and seek revenge.

LIFE CYCLE: 101 days under the curse, or a lifetime, until cured, killed, or passed on.

HISTORY: Accounts of Rougarou go all the way back to medieval France.

Through the 1600s, the condition was believed to be hereditary, with the one afflicted leading a normal life, unsuspecting until something triggered the transformation changing their physique and leaving them with a hunger for raw meat. The change was not complete unless they took a bite of human flesh.

One of the most notable cases, from France in the late 1700s, tells of one that has come to be known as the Beast of Gévaudan. This Rougarou terrorized the region for three years, said to have slaughtered between sixty and one hundred people before being put down by three bullets made from a melted-down silver baptismal chalice that had been blessed.

Some accounts, however, have no basis in French culture. In the Louisiana region of the early 1700s, the Attakapa were at war with the Opelousas and the Chitimacha tribes. This native tribe was known for its blood-thirsty nature and for consuming human flesh. When they lost their war, the few survivors fled into the swamp, where it is said they encountered an evil spirit that possessed them, granting them the power to shapeshift. Legend says that the Attakapa embraced their bestial nature and cravings for human flesh and blood, becoming the Wolf-Walkers terrorizing the region.

Southern Louisiana, the territory of the Rougarou, has been plagued by animal mutilations and strange, violent deaths as recently as the mid-to-late 2010s. Some accounts have reached as far as Texas, Colorado, and Alabama.

artist's rendition of a Sewer Blob

Sewer Blob

ORIGINS: In dank, dark places all around the world lurk strange, amorphous, pulsating blob-like beasts. Very little is known about these gelatinous orbs. On the two occasions when video proof of this rare creature was released to the public, the scientific community could not agree on its origin.

Some individuals theorize they are otherworldly beings, others, evolved slime molds, or mutated beasts. Positive identification has proven elusive as no direct human contact has been confirmed.

LIFE CYCLE: Unknown.

HISTORY: In December 2007, a blob-like mass was discovered in the Crestview Water System in Denver, Colorado.

The creature was captured on video secured by a remote camera fed into the sewers for surveillance.

A specialist from the Colorado Division of Wildlife explained the gelatinous mass to be a bryozoan colony, but this theory is not supported by the image in the video.

Bryozoan colonies generally have a fan-like appearance or an exoskeleton made of chitin. Other colonies look like small corals, or can resemble an open head of lettuce. No form of bryozoan is capable of the pulsating movement shown in the video.

Again, in April of 2009, in the sewers beneath Cameron Village in Raleigh, North Carolina, high-tech cameras again discovered an amorphous, pulsating blob-like beast.

A staff biologist from the Raleigh Public Utilities Department identified the creature as a colony of Tubifax worms, while a biology professor from a nearby University again identified it as colony of bryozoans.

However, a bryozoan expert with the Department of Biological Sciences at Wright State University in Dayton, Ohio claimed the blob was clumps of annelid worms.

None of these explanations can explain how the mass is able to pulsate and move in the manner shown in the videos.

To this day, the sewer blob defies alternate identification.

SHADOW PEOPLE

(Also known as Hat Man, The Hooded Monk, Old Hag, Black Smoke People, Peeking Shadows, Red-Eyed Shadows, Tariaksuq, The Watchers, Mist People, and various other names worldwide.)

ORIGINS: While theories abound, nothing definitive has been settled on as the origin of the Shadow People. Some of the most popular theories on the nature and origin of Shadow People are as follows:

They are other-dimensional beings; they are time travelers; they are the early stage of emergent demons; they are guardian angels; they are developing doppelgangers; they are extraterrestrial in nature; they are the aura of an individual scrying the victim.

From a scientific rationale, Shadow People are hallucinations stemming from several possible scenarios. The first is sleep paralysis, or Paradoxical Sleep, where chemicals in the brain freeze the body's muscles during REM sleep so that the sleeper does not physically act out their dreams during sleep. A person can wake before the chemicals have cleared from their body. Sleep paralysis can occur when falling asleep or waking and produces the symptoms conversant with a visitation. The second is Pareidolia, the human mind's ability to see shapes or pictures in randomness.

Some theorize these effects are caused by the abuse of the stimulant methamphetamine, which—due to prolonged sleep deprivation—can be the cause of hallucinations matching the description of Shadow People, or mental conditions such as schizophrenia or bipolar disorder, which can cause a similar perception of shadowy figures in the subject's peripheral vision. There are even some theories that this effect is caused by sound, or to be precise, infrasound, which is of low enough frequency that the human ear cannot hear it but is known to affect both mind and body.

DESCRIPTION: Accounts depict the Shadow People as solid black humanoid masses that appear at the foot of the bed or in the corner of the room. Height varies from child-sided to taller than normal. They move with fast, jerky motions and can pass through solid matter, often disappearing through walls or mirrors. Some wear hats, and some wear cloaks. All basically have a human shape but are only defined from the waist up. The legs generally fade in an approximation of those appendages to the floor. When

artist's rendition of a Shadow Person

they are seen moving, they have been described as gliding rather than walking.

In most cases, the Shadow Person is featureless, like a silhouette but with substance, though some accounts mention the beings as semi-transparent.

If a feature is mentioned, it is generally the eyes, which can be of varying colors, perhaps linked to the particular nature of that entity, such as red eyes being malevolent and white eyes being benevolent. To this effect, some believe Shadow People are actually demonic beings, and the more powerful they get, the less distinct their shape becomes.

Though there is no indication of Shadow People attempting to verbally communicate, some say that if you look at their chest or eyes, they scream, making a sound like static, wind, or wood creaking.

Reports have been documented of a great sense of fear or malevolence. Whether this stems from the creature or the experience is unclear. Some people feel the Shadow People are parasitic beings there to feed off fear; others believe they are guardian spirits that mean no harm.

It is common in the accounts where the person has the experience during sleep to exhibit paralysis and heaviness, including difficulty breathing as if they are being smothered or someone is on their chest. In many cases, those reporting the encounter express being overcome with a sense of dread or fear. Others have had a sensation of having someone sit beside them, having their blankets pulled away, or being touched. Some say they have a black spot where they were touched that did not go away for years.

In almost all cases, the person experiencing the visitation described merely being watched, with the Shadow Person going away as soon as they were noticed.

There have also been cases reported of people observing Shadow People, or occasionally Shadow Animals, in the daylight hours, both inside and outside, such as hiding behind a bush or moving down stairs. Some cases of sightings seem tied to a particular location, but others seem tied to an individual, with the episodes following them sometimes clear to other states.

Another variation equated with Shadow People is a glowing white orb that will likewise disappear by passing through solid matter.

LIFE CYCLE: Undetermined.

HISTORY: Shadow People are one of the first identified cryptids in recorded history, with sightings documented for thousands of years worldwide, with variants found in every culture and religion. Those accounts show startling similarity, regardless of period or location.

In 1887, the French author Guy de Maupassant wrote the story "Le Horla" about shadow beings with similarities to depictions of Shadow People.

The term itself was first used in 1953 as the title of a radio drama broadcast on a Chicago station. In April of 2001, another late-night radio show revitalized the belief in Shadow People, and later that year, a book titled The Secret War was written about them.

As recent as 2010, Shadow People were the most regularly reported paranormal occurrence in America.

VARIATIONS: Some of the cryptids Shadow People have also been equated with are the Bogeyman, the Raven Mocker, and the Djinn, all creatures that take black, shadowy form.

artist's rendition of a Skadegamutc

Skadegamutc

(Also known as a Ghost Witch)

ORIGINS: This is a blood-sucking creature from the lore of the Wabanaki, or People of the Dawnland, an alliance of tribes located in Maine that still exist today. It is said that those who practice black magic come back after death as this type of vampire, though contrary to other vampire lore, they do not retain a healthy, youthful appearance, instead showing the decay of death.

DESCRIPTION: During the daylight hours the ghost witch appears as one would expect a corpse to look, with decaying or desiccated flesh and evidence of any injuries that lead to their death. At night they transform to a glowing orb that travels through the darkness looking for humans to prey upon. By some accounts they can transform back to their zombie state and feed. To maintain their existence they must consume flesh and blood. They are said to retain their magical abilities and are reported to cast curses on those they encounter.

They have two ways they typically attack. The first is to prey on the grief-stricken, hovering near open-air burials waiting for the mourners to rest, which is when they strike. The second is to fly around looking for travelers who have been separated from their group. When they find them, they swoop down and quietly feed.

In their undead form they cannot be harmed, except if burned to ash and the remains scattered.

LIFE CYCLE: As this cryptid results from the death of a practitioner of black magic, it cannot be said to be a life cycle, but sorcerers who refuse to stay dead come back as this creature.

HISTORY: Among the tribes there are stories of those who encountered this creature, notably one couple traveling through the woods who chose to shelter in a grove where a magician had been put to rest in the treetops. Despite the wife's reluctance, they bedded down for the night. The wife woke to a gnawing sound that had disturbed her sleep all night. When she went to wake her husband his left side had been eaten away, including his heart. She went to the townfolk for help. When she told her horrific story, they lowered the magician's corpse from the treetop to discover blood on its face.

artist's rendition of a Skinwalker

SKINWALKER

(Also called Yee naaldlooshii, which translates into "with it, he goes on all fours" in the language of the Diné — or Navajo.)

ORIGINS: Versions of human shapshifters exist around the world. In North America, there are among the native tribes multiple versions of what are called skinwalkers. These are witches that have joined the secret society of skinwalkers by violating cultural and sacred taboos, performing a ritual dance meant to curse rather than heal to gain power and magic for selfish ends.

The highest rank of these witches completes an act such as cannibalism, incest, or killing a close blood relative to attain their power.

DESCRIPTION: Skinwalkers have the ability to become any animal they chose by donning the creature's pelt, though they can change without doing so. Because of this, the Navajo have a cultural taboo against wearing furs, particularly those of predators.

Often skinwalkers are said to appear as coyotes, crows, wolves, or other predators, but they can choose the form to suit their current needs. They can even appear as another human being by stealing the face of the person. Their ability to transform can also extend to their voice, allowing them to lure victims with what sounds like a baby crying or a loved one's voice.

Whatever form they take on, one can recognize them in their transformed state by their supernatural speed, their malformed shape, and their glowing animal eyes. To meet that unnatural gaze is to give the witch power over you.

It is also said that to say the word skinwalker is to draw their attention to you, so they are not talked about openly or among non-native individuals.

LIFE CYCLE: Unknown.

HISTORY: Due to the cultural taboo against speaking of this creature, there are not a lot of specific accounts, beyond the events at Sherman — or Skinwalker — Ranch, in Ballad, Utah, but there have been many accounts of coyotes and other animals pacing cars at great speeds on secluded roadways, and behaving in other unnatural ways.

SNALLYGASTER

(From the German Schneller Geist meaning "quick spirit." Also known as a "sky beast" by Native American nations.)

ORIGINS: This cryptid was first sighted in Frederick County at the beginning of the 20th century. It is believed to be a reappearance of creatures encountered by the German immigrants that settled in the Blue Ridge Mountains in the early 18th century who were terrorized by a creature they referred to as Schneller Geist, or quick spirit.

Slaves were warned against escape lest they encounter the snallygasters in their flight.

The only known protections against this creature are avoidance, and a seven-pointed star called a hex sign, such as those found on many barns in Pennsylvania Dutch country.

It is said the Dwayyo, another Maryland region cryptid, are their mortal enemies.

There are some theories that the snallygaster may be related to similar creatures cited in Native American lore.

DESCRIPTION: Though many eyewitness accounts vary, it is generally agreed that this large flying creature is part avian and part reptile, with wings spanning at least twelve to fourteen feet and stood to a height of up to twenty feet. By comparison, it was estimated to be the size of an dirigible. In some accounts, the snallygaster has a long, needle-like beak, claws and teeth like steel, and a tail twenty feet long. Other features cited are fur instead of feathers, horns, tentacles, and dragon-like aspects.

There is some debate whether the snallygaster has monocular or binocular vision. Some theorize that the creature may have had the chameleon-like ability to alter not just its form, but also its size and color. The cries of the snallygaster range from a shrill screech to a blood-curdling roar to a whistle said to be similar to a locomotive. A snallygaster was reported to have killed a man by piercing his neck and sucking his blood. They are also known to carry off both children and cattle.

LIFE CYCLE: The life expectancy of a snallygaster is believed to be no more than twenty years. There are several accounts of the discovery of nests and eggs, generally on cliff faces at a great height, though early records denote a preference for nesting in caves.

The young are hatched from massive eggs large enough to produce offspring the size of a horse

artist's rendition of a Snallygaster

or an elephant. It is not known if the young hatch dependent, as with avian offspring; or self-sufficient, as with reptilian young.

HISTORY: There are some claims that early media coverage was a hoax, but sightings and accounts continued well into the mid-twentieth century.

A resurgence of sightings in Frederick County began in 1909, as cited in Middletown's Valley Register, but were not limited to this region. There were accounts of encounters all over Maryland, as well as Ohio, Washington DC, West Virginia, and New Jersey.

Accounts of the snallygaster have also been featured in the Baltimore Sun, National Geographic, and Time Magazine, and in 1976, The Washington Post sponsored a search for the snallygaster and other regional cryptids.

The Smithsonian offered a $100,000 reward for the hide of a snallygaster, and by some accounts, President Theodore Roosevelt considered hunting the beast.

Evidence for the existence of this cryptid was reported in 1932, when the skeletal remains of a snallygaster were found in a mash vat in a moonshine factory in Hagerstown, Maryland. Before these remains could be recovered, revenue agents destroyed the vat with dynamite.

Although no sightings have been reported in recent years, they are still believed to be active in the mountains of western Maryland, especially around Frederick County.

artist's rendition of a Van Meter Visitor

VAN METER VISITOR

ORIGINS: A regional cryptid, the Van Meter Visitor hails from the state of Iowa. First sighted in Van Meter in 1903, there have been reports of other encounters in the state as recently as 2020.

DESCRIPTION: Depending on the account, the Van Meter Visitor has been described as a winged bipedal half-human, half-animal creature standing as much as nine feet tall, or presenting as five feet long in flight. The wings are described as bat-like, but the creature is also said to resemble a modern spoonbill or a pterodactyl. By some accounts, the wings were large enough to obscure the sky when flapping.

Other than its grand stature, this cryptid is described as having a horn protruding from its forehead that emits a beam of light, and the creature emanates a powerful stench said to disrupt the thoughts and memory of those nearby.

A plaster cast was made of a three-toed clawed depression believed to be its footprint. Some witnesses claimed that it hopped like a kangaroo, but others said it moved with great speed across the rooftops.

Though multiple people reported firing guns at the creature, they claim it was to no effect.

LIFE CYCLE: While there are no specific details about the creature's reproduction, there have been sightings of multiple Visitors of varying sizes, making plausible the consideration that a population exists, whether the variance in size denotes young or gendered individuals, there is insufficient data to determine.

HISTORY: The original encounter is documented to have taken place in Van Meter, Iowa, in September and October of 1903. Over the course of five nights, multiple well-respected individuals reportedly engaged with the Van Meter Visitor.

When the sightings continued, the residents of the town formed a posse and tracked the creatures to a nearby abandoned mine. At the first the creatures flew off; when they returned, they descended into the mine, ignoring those firing upon them.

Though the townfolk left no further documentation of encounters, there have been other reports.

One such encounter took place near the abandoned mine in the 1980, where new residents out for a walk reported a massive, bird-like creature flying overhead.

In 2000, a family driving home to Van Meter reported seeing a corpse of a Visitor on the side of the road, but when the father went back to look, it was gone.

Other such occurrences have been reported in the nearby area as recently as 2020.

While there are theories as to the true nature of the Van Meter Visitor, including but not limited to the possibility of misidentification, it being an undiscovered species, and the belief that it is a trans-dimensional being, any true determination cannot be reached without further evidence.

WAMPUS CAT

(Also known as Catawampus, Wampus Beast, Cherokee Death Cat)

ORIGINS: The Wampus Cat is mostly sighted in the Appalachians and the South, but there are accounts it also hails from Texas, Idaho, Tennessee, West Virginia, the Carolinas, and Washington state. A couple variations of the lore are rooted in native Cherokee legends, but are also attributed to tales told by lumberjacks, likely to keep folk out of the woods.

DESCRIPTION: A nocturnal cat-like creature with an affinity for water, sometimes described as half cat and half dog. It is reported to have glowing yellow or green eyes that can pierce the soul, driving a person insane. It is also said that under a full moon they can start forest fires with no more than a glare. Some call it a water-panther and describe it as black as dusk. It is known for having a loud, terrible voice, but also for being able to change how it sounds to mimic other creatures. Other accounts tell of tufted ears, sharp claws, an unholy stench, and shedding whiskers that are white during the day and black at night. Another defining feature is a right arm like a folding pruning hook, used to snatch prey from the sky, particularly eagles. Depending on the account, it is the size of a Maine Coon, or it stands five feet tall on its hind legs. There are those who say it is bipedal. Others say it has three sets of legs.

In some versions, the Wampus is half-woman, half-cat, with occult powers and shapeshifting abilities. It is said her high-pitched howl is a harbinger of death. When someone hears it, they will lose someone within three days.

There are a lot of wild claims attributed to the Wampus Cat, including curdling sourdough, stealing miners' picks to clean its teeth, marking false trails through the mountains with its claws, and chasing fish from the river by walking through the water.

LIFE CYCLE: Unknown.

HISTORY: The Wampus Cat has been blamed for slaughtering livestock since the early 19th century and there have been sightings ever since, generally late at night in rural areas. Some claim she is a witch living alone in the mountains, transforming into the beast to steal chicken and pigs.

There are also two Cherokee legends said to be the origin of Wampus Cat. In the first, a suspicious or curious wife puts on a mountain lion skin to spy on her

artist's rendition of a Wampus Cat

husband and other men from the tribe as they perform a ritual to prepare for the hunt. When she is discovered, the shaman curses her to live as the Wampus Cat forever, fusing the skin with her flesh. In the other legend a fierce warrior goes out into the night to fight a creature called the Ewah that has terrorized the village. He comes back mad, a mere shell of himself. His wife goes to the shaman for help getting revenge on the creature. They give her a bobcat mask and cover her scent with a black paste. When she sneaks up on the Ewah, the sight of her mask turns the creature' magic on itself, banishing it forever. The woman's spirit is said to now inhabit the Wampus Cat as she continues to protect her village.

Hunters are still reporting encounters with the Wampus to this day.

artist's rendition of a Wunk

Wunk

ORIGINS: The Wunk is known first and foremost among the lumberjack communities of the United States. Due to the nature of the Wunk, it has not been proven if this creature exists, or if it evolved from the practice of hazing new immigrants.

DESCRIPTION: A creature of the forest known for curiosity but also for being extremely shy. With no confirmed sightings, the creature's physical description has not been documented. While it watches those around it, when sighted, it retreats, not merely running away, but digging a hole in the ground to disappear into. Once in the hole, it pulls the edges in after itself, leaving no trace.

It is said to have the ability to transform into any creature and appear indistinguishable from the original, animal or human. By some accounts, the Wunk does not actually make use of this ability to escape detection, but it is also posited that if it did, how would the observer know? In either case, because of its particular nature, Wunk sightings are largely unreported and/or unrealized.

LIFE CYCLE: Unknown.

HISTORY: Earliest mention of the Wunk appear in the late 19th to early 20th century.

VARIATIONS:

Squidgicum-Squee

ORIGINS: Also know among the lumberjack communities of the United States in the late 19th and early 20th centuries.

DESCRIPTION: The Squidgicum-Squee is accounted to be a big-mouthed creature with what appear to be trees growing out of its back. Rather than digging holes to hide in, this cryptid opens its mouth wide, breaths in deeply, and swallows itself whole.

There is no confirmation that these two creatures are related, but the similarities between them are noteworthy.

artist's rendition of a Squidgicum-Squee

About the Author

Award-winning author, editor, and publisher **Danielle Ackley-McPhail** has worked both sides of the publishing industry for longer than she cares to admit. In 2014 she joined forces with Mike McPhail and Greg Schauer to form eSpec Books.

Her published works include eight novels: *Yesterday's Dreams, Tomorrow's Memories, Today's Promise, The Halfling's Court, The Redcaps' Queen, Daire's Devils, The Play of Light,* and *Baba Ali and the Clockwork Djinn,* written with Day Al-Mohamed. She is also the author of the solo collections *Eternal Wanderings, A Legacy of Stars, Consigned to the Sea, Flash in the Can, Transcendence, The Kindly Ones, Dawns a New Day, The Fox's Fire, Between Darkness and Light, Echoes of the Divine,* and the non-fiction writers' guides *The Literary Handyman, More Tips from the Handyman, LH: Build-A-Book Workshop,* and *The Literary Handyman Library* omnibus edition. She is the senior editor of the *Bad-Ass Faeries* anthology series, *No Longer Dreams, Heroes of the Realm, Clockwork Chaos, Gaslight & Grimm, Grimm Machinations, A Cast of Crows, A Cry of Hounds, Other Aether, The Chaos Clock, Grease Monkeys, Side of Good/Side of Evil, After Punk,* and *Footprints in the Stars.* Her short stories are included in numerous other anthologies and collections. She is a full member of the Science Fiction and Fantasy Writers Association and a Supporting Ally in the Horror Writers Association.

Until his decades-long disappearance, **JW Harp** was known for his trippy underground comic strip *Captain Thetan*, about a seafarer who controls reality for himself and others. This otherworldly character appeared in a dozen issues of the classic rare underground zine *Sandanista Romp*. JW has reemerged thanks largely to eSpec Books' Systema Paradoxa series. In 2023, JW started Skilletfire Studios with comic-book author Scott Eckelaert. Under the Skilletfire Studios mantle, JW has produced the graphic novel *Boylon Heights*, and the *Gimme Five Comics* series. Since its launch, *Gimme Five Comics* has included work by Artyom Topilin, Elena Cerisciola, John L. French, Keith Lansdale, and Joe R. Lansdale with more to come.

JW grew up in the seedy parts of South Carolina, which is all of it. He feels part Canadian and part Costa Rican these days. He lives in North Carolina. Please get in touch with him at jwharp@skilletfire.com.

CAPTURE THE CRYPTIDS!

Cryptid Crate is a monthly subscription box filled with various cryptozoology and paranormal-themed items to wear, display, and collect. Expect a carefully curated box filled with creeptastic pieces from indie makers and artisans pertaining to bigfoot, sasquatch, UFOs, ghosts, and other cryptid and mysterious creatures (apparel, decor, media, etc).

Now Featuring Cryptid Crate Jr!

http://CryptidCrate.com